THE GUARDIANS OF ETERNITY

Gaurika Singh

Chennai • Bangalore

CLEVER FOX PUBLISHING
Chennai, India

Published by CLEVER FOX PUBLISHING 2024
Copyright © Gaurika Singh 2024

All Rights Reserved.
ISBN: 978-93-56485-73-0

This book has been published with all reasonable efforts taken to make the material error-free after the consent of the author. No part of this book shall be used, reproduced in any manner whatsoever without written permission from the author, except in the case of brief quotations embodied in critical articles and reviews.

The Author of this book is solely responsible and liable for its content including but not limited to the views, representations, descriptions, statements, information, opinions and references ["Content"]. The Content of this book shall not constitute or be construed or deemed to reflect the opinion or expression of the Publisher or Editor. Neither the Publisher nor Editor endorse or approve the Content of this book or guarantee the reliability, accuracy or completeness of the Content published herein and do not make any representations or warranties of any kind, express or implied, including but not limited to the implied warranties of merchantability, fitness for a particular purpose. The Publisher and Editor shall not be liable whatsoever for any errors, omissions, whether such errors or omissions result from negligence, accident, or any other cause or claims for loss or damages of any kind, including without limitation, indirect or consequential loss or damage arising out of use, inability to use, or about the reliability, accuracy or sufficiency of the information contained in this book.

PREFACE

*I*n the vast expanse of literary creation, there exists a realm where stories are forged, characters come to life, and the boundaries of imagination are pushed to their limits. Within the pages of "Guardians of Eternity," I invite you to embark on a journey that transcends time, where the echoes of ancient pacts and the whispers of forbidden knowledge weave a tapestry of intrigue and adventure.

At the heart of this saga lie three figures, emerging from the shadows of history: Epsita, Raunav, and Vikram. Bound by a pact steeped in darkness, they set forth on a malevolent quest to seize control of the ultimate power: immortality. Their journey takes them through the sacred grounds of the nine realms, each housing a gem infused with the arcane secrets of Mrit Sanjeevani Vidya – the elusive path to eternal life.

As our protagonists traverse perilous landscapes and challenge the very forces of nature, they leave behind a wake of chaos and destruction. Their pursuit of immortality knows no bounds as they manipulate, deceive, and betray all who stand in their path.

Yet, with each step closer to eternal life, they risk losing their very essence to the darkness that lurks within. For as they delve deeper into the forbidden knowledge of the gems, they awaken ancient evils that threaten to consume them.

"Guardians of Eternity" is more than a tale; it is a saga of villainy, ambition, and the seduction of power. Within these pages, the lines between good and evil blur, and the boundaries of morality are tested against the allure of absolute power.

As you journey through the pages of this epic, may you find yourself drawn into a world where the guardians of eternity tread a fine line between salvation and damnation. Will Epsita, Raunav, and Vikram achieve their nefarious goal and attain immortality? Or will their insatiable thirst for power lead to their ultimate downfall, plunging the world into eternal darkness?

Prepare to be enthralled by a tale that challenges the very fabric of existence, where the guardians of eternity hold the key to the fate of the world.

Welcome to "Guardians of Eternity."

-Gaurika Singh

CONTENTS

Preface *3*

1. The first step 6
2. The Dark Lord 10
3. Who's favorable: Devil or Divine? 14
4. Vengeance overtakes consciousness. 20
5. Not Just a Mountain 26
6. Old feuds 32
7. The divine metamorphosis 38
8. The Arrival 46
9. The Tax of Love 52
10. The Betrayal 62
11. The unknown? 74
12. It is not over yet 82
13. Another Traitor 88
14. It's Not Over Yet 100

Acknowledgement *103*

CHAPTER 1

THE FIRST STEP

The first step

YEAR 2140

An awkward silence surrounded Vikram and Epsita, where Vikram just sipped his last sip of tea and kept the cup on the table, well the cup for sure reflected Epsita's richness as she served tea in an ancient kubachi teacup decorated with a 2-carat emerald on the tip of the shaft of the stirring spoon.

While Vikram had his sight stuck on the opulent view of the teacup he was disturbed by a thin voice, which was of Epsita, as she asked, "Vikram, I have got to know that you were looking for nemala sarsen which was the last sarsen made in the area of Stonehenge during the bronze age of humanity. Well, being a wife of an archaeologist, I am aware that according to the radiocarbon- dating of nemala, its formation matches the year when kali-yuga started (the peak of Dvapara-Yuga) about 5121 years ago from the year 2020."

Vikram was surprised by knowing that Epsita was not only a rich beautiful woman but a truly knowledgeable lady who could help Vikram with his mysteries to solve and help him to unlock the doors of boon for Vikram.

What can the boon be? How is it fruitful for Vikram? Lastly, why is he expecting Epsita to be a source?

All these questions shall be answered in the upcoming events and dynamic scenarios which will take p l a c e .

After some silence, Vikram couldn't stop himself from praising Epsita and continued by saying in a subtle tone, "Well Epsita! I am quite impressed of your knowledge on this topic because not everyone is aware of this vital information."

Epsita smiled, but in the next instant she gave a confused look to Vikram, which was indeed, noticeably clear to Vikram

and so, he said, "Epsita I understand, that you are still thinking about the purpose of my arrival to your place, but for now that wouldn't be important to be known to you, I have a series of important information to be given to you in order to revive some of the happenings you might even remember."

"What do you mean? Is it, some crisis like covid or something more dangerous, that might have happened?" Epsita asked out of pure confusion.

"Uhmm, that is not the case it is something related to our pasts in Yugas. You must be surprised to know but I have some tricks which have made me capable to know the exact happenings in the past." Vikram explains.

The first step

"Oh, that seems exciting, let's see what have you got." Epsita exclaimed.

Vikram starts narrating a piece of story, which connects no dots but makes Epsita gain interest.

CHAPTER 2

THE DARK LORD

*I*t was an empty open auditorium of ancient times, where the pendulum-like structure stood 160 meters high, ticking just forever without even skipping a beat. It was the only way the locals could know the number of days which had passed as it rang quite loudly, be it night or day, it is certain that the laws of pendulum to go on forever was discovered way back, than what we know now. Amidst the ticking clock-like pendulum and the eerie silence which was mixed with the screeching of an owl during the night, there was something else being cooked up in the crowd of perfectionists and innocents, a person who was living with a goal to disrupt the tranquility that the locals had established to make an ideal world we expect now in this century. There was something more than just silence, serenity, cleanliness physically and mentally amongst the crowd of the people living in the golden age of humanity also known as, 'The Satya Yuga.' (Rusted door made of iron makes a creaking noise as opened to enter the auditorium.)

"It is supposed to be here, I saw it here trust me." said Narottama the local's head, bowing his head Infront of one hundred feet tall black silhouette.

A voice filled with boldness and utter rage then echoed in the auditorium almost choking Narottama by his neck and said," they are all gone it was supposed to be here." the silhouette then took a deep breath composing himself, but his eyes were still red with fury as if whoever confronts him will face death and be slaughtered by the inhumane figure that appeared in the auditorium.

While Vikram was narrating, Epsita interrupted and said," what are these people referring to what is not there in the auditorium? Who is this figure, who is filled with brutality even after taking birth in the golden age of humanity? Vikram why don't you clarify?"

Vikram grasped the glass of water which was kept covered since the start of his narration covered with silver plate on its top. He gulped the water which slid down his throat, which was clearly visible to Epsita. He had sweat trickling down his forehead even after the AC's were on, then he collected himself from the sense of fear he faced and replied," I know you are curious to know everything, but I would be answering only one of your questions as the other one should be known to you as I proceed. So, the figure whose height was about 100 feet was nobody else but, Shukracharya himself."

"WHAT!!! SHUKRACHARYA???? HOWW? WHEN? GRACIOUS! HOW DO YOU KNOW ALL OF THIS WHO ARE YOU?" Epsita was shocked from the core of her heart after hearing the name Shukracharya as if she already knew something negative about him and couldn't believe Vikram taking his name.

What was so creepy about Shukracharya that scared Epsita to the core?

__To be unveiled in the upcoming mysteries of the dark lord 'Shukracharya.'__

CHAPTER 3

WHO'S FAVORABLE: DEVIL OR DIVINE?

$\mathcal{V}$ikram tried to calm Epsita down by giving her a glass of water, and continued," I hope you are, ok?"

Epsita nodded in agreement and looked towards the kubachi teacup for a second and looked back at Vikram when he interrupted and asked," what made you so restless? Are you already familiar to this name?"

Epsita gulped the water in fear and said smiling in doubt," Actually when I was a child my father used to tell me a story of the lord of devils, who's one and only goal was to get the 9 words-crafted sentence to spread negativity, so, I just thought that what if the story was actually true rather than just a fiction tale to scare me and you could have been the carrier of negativity to help Shukracharya."

She smiled in guilt and bowed her head slightly to apologize.

Vikram laughed and said," that's very naïve of you but it is true that Shukracharya was looking for 9 words-crafted sentence in order to make all the negative powers immortal."

"Really? But even after Shukracharya is the brother of goddess Lakshmi, grandson of lord brahma himself, still he chose the path to lead the asuras. Why so?"

Vikram tried to satisfy the fire of curiosity which had just ignited in Epsita by telling the history of Asura

Guru Shukracharya," Shukra is a Sanskrit word which means, cleanliness and purity, but unlike his name he was something of an enigma, he had each and every mighty tool from which he could gain any divine power of the world no matter how strong it could be. It was Shukra was in his 20's when he was meditating on the edge land of Roop Kund, to gain the boon of Mrit Sanjeevini vidya by lord shiva himself, he saw th*ese words appear in the blanks of his eyes, as if he just saw a prediction of Kaliyuga.*

"कैलाशपर्वतस्य विभूतिमाणि शृङ्गाणि, एकलः सः तिष्ठति सर्वसमर्थः।

कदापि न कोऽपि तस्य आरोहितवान्, बालिका एका कलियुगे जानीत।

रहस्यानि सर्वाणि प्रकटयिष्यति, सा गोप्यमेवाखिलं विकशिष्यति।"

"What does that even mean?" Epsita asked hesitantly. Vikram felt interrupted for a second, but then he composed himself and said," It was in a form of poem which meant:

Amidst the grandeur of Kailash's heights so vast,

There stands a solitary, unwavering mast.

No other can ascend without a doubt,

But there's one girl, a secret's key throughout.

In this age of Kaal, she shall unfurl,

All hidden mysteries, as if a precious pearl."

"Oh! All right, you continue." Epsita exclaimed.

Vikram continued from where he left," Shukra was bewildered, of an unexpected prediction which had just laid in its entirety on the frames of his eyes. But before he could interpret what had just happened, he realized that he wasn't hungry anymore and the open cuts on his body weren't visible; when he opened his eyes in wonder, he found himself sunk in the aura of a bright golden light, illuminating each and every corner of Roop Kund, he squinted his eyes in order to see the source from which huge masses of light chunks fell before his eyes, once his sight pierced into such strong aura, he saw a man holding a trident with his right hand. The man Infront of him had a radiant skin, which could have been seen from miles away, he wore a tiger pelt also known as 'Vyaghra Charma' in Sanskrit, he was covered with Bhasma which is basically a powder-like substance made of corpse bones, which glorified his looks even more. Epsita, you know whom I am talking about, right?"

Epsita smirked and said," Of course, it was nobody else but lord shiva himself."

Vikram smiled back and said," Exactly! After years of Tap yoga Shukra finally felt himself and almost cried after seeing his deity in his entirety, Shukra wiped his tears and sobbed while praising the majestic looks of lord shiva, which was inexplicable for sure. Shukra was still in the process of rebounding himself, a deep voice pierced through his soul; as Shukra looked up, he saw that lord shiva himself gave his auspice and realized that he shouldn't waste his time by rebounding from the grand and majestic scene he saw and while he was thinking this lord shiva spoke," My dear child you have completed 3 Shahashtra years (3000 years) of your Tapasya, ask me whatever you want, I shall grant you the righteous boon for your struggles you faced all these years, while chanting my name."

"Oh, majesty of mine! I have been starving, covered with termites for all these years, these termites gradually savored my flesh, making me look no lesser than a beast, but nothing could stop me from chanting your name. So, hey Shiva, I ask you to bless me with Mrit Sanjeevini Vidya."

"Tathastu (Granted)" said lord shiva and granted what Shukra had always wanted and after he was titled as Shukracharya"

Epsita interrupted once again and said," The end? Why did Shukracharya even ask for such a useless boon which could help him in no manner? It was better if he would have asked for salvation or immortality or even a place in one of the Lokas."

Vikram was indeed agitated by Epsita's behavior as she was behaving as if she had taken an oath to not let anyone finish their sentence.

But we know that she had a point in asking this. Well, we know that there is nothing superior to having a place in one of the Lokas, then what forced Shukracharya to ask for Mrit Sanjeevani Vidya over other fruitful boons.

CHAPTER 4

VENGEANCE OVERTAKES CONSCIOUSNESS.

Vengeance overtakes consciousness.

*I*t was the last straw and Vikram was pissed off, he said in a cold manner, "EPSITA! Stop interrupting please."

Epsita was embarrassed and so she apologized.

It could not really calm Vikram down, but he functioned as if he had accepted her apologies and answered her calmly, "So, let us talk about Shukracharya's past or the time before he went to Roop Kund. It was the time when Shukracharya with other devas was gaining all kinds of education; be it astra vidya (education of how to use weapons), shastrartha (Debate), kundalini Jagriti Vidya (Activating indris by meditation) and many more. Shukracharya proved himself to be far better than the devas, in a nutshell he was a prodigy, but guru Brihaspati was quite biased towards the devas and never paid attention towards the blooming prodigy. This caused vengeance towards the devas to ignite in Shukracharya's heart and brain. The situation went south, when lord Vishnu himself gave his full support to the devas, it truly pissed off Shukracharya, and so he decided to lead the army of asuras. Since then, started the game of vengeance. As Shukracharya was against lord Vishnu, he taught the asuras all the ways they can be attacked and how to counter the Astras. Even after the Asuras new all the techniques that the Devas would use on them, they were not strong enough and used to die a painful death. This caused Shukracharya to ask for Mrit Sanjeevani Vidya as a boon from Lord Shiva. The Devas were immortal, and Shukracharya had the most vital key for his victory, 'The Mrit Sanjeevani,' with this the asuras used to be brought back from death. This caused an endless war between the Asuras and the Devas

To resist such endless wars, Lord Vishnu himself went to Lord Shiva, and insisted on removing Shukracharya's memory of Mrit Sanjeevani Vidya, so that he could not revive the asuras and encourage them to fight the Devas. Lord shiva showed an expression of regret and helplessness, as once a boon is granted to the person who asked for it, cannot be taken back. Well, this doesn't mean it was the end.

Lord shiva knew that if he divides Shukracharya's memory about Mrit Sanjeevani into nine portions and hide all those 9 portions in 9 different gemstones, and just so he did, all the asuras received salvation from their bodies or simply deh.

This made Shukracharya restless, and he knew that the reason for Vishnu's triumph was the sudden memory loss of the Mrit Sanjeevani Vidya, being a prodigy of his childhood, he knew that Mrit Sanjeevani Vidya has nine streams, each of which when joined together forms distinct types of gemstones. At the same time, Lord shiva threw all these gemstones in different directions of mount Kailash in such a way that each of them falls in a lake.

Vengeance overtakes consciousness.

Shukracharya saw nine different shooting stars-like gems falling in different direction. He rushed and noted the exact place into which they had fallen."

Epsita once again in wonder, said," If Shukracharya knew where the gems had fallen, then why didn't he go and picked them, instead of just noting where they had fallen?"

Vikram replied," Because he couldn't just go and pick them up, as these gemstones were no ordinary gems but spelled gems."

"Spelled gems?" Epsita asked in wonder.

"Yes, spelled gems, Once the process of dividing each 9 sectors of Mrit Sanjeevani into gems was completed, Lord Shiva made each gem an encrypted one, each sector of Mrit Sanjeevani which were now gems, locked with mantras which had to be activated in order to bring back the respective sector of Mrit Sanjeevani Vidya." Vikram took a break and sipped the leftover water which was kept on the table.

"Wow! System of numerical and alphabetical locks is so ancient." Epsita laughed while uttering these words and asked Vikram to have some sweets that came as *Prasad* from Kailash darshan itself.

Vikram held the sweet in his hand and stared at it while smiling continuously and slowly engulfed it in huge chunks.

"Is there a story for this sweet too, that you are smiling so hard." Epsita asked in a taunting manner.

Vikram devoured his last bite and then replied," Unfortunately I don't have any story for this scrumptious thing, but I do have a mystery to be unfurled from where this sweet came from."

To be continued ....

CHAPTER 5

NOT JUST A MOUNTAIN

"So, I definitely made a right guess of you having something in your mind." Epsita proudly declared.

Vikram smiled and continued," Till now, I was telling you about Shukracharya's history and how he was related to Mrit Sanjeevani and why he did not pick the gems. Now let me unlock the mysteries of mount Kailash where Shukracharya went, to keep an eye on the gems. Now Kailash is called the point where heaven meets earth or in other words the pivotal point of earth. Why? You ask."

Vikram turned his laptop's screen towards Epsita. After seeing all those numbers, she was surprised to know why we call Kailash is called the Centre of the Earth.

The screen displayed;

Distance between:

North pole and Kailash- 6666 km

South pole and Kailash- 13,332 km

Kailash and Stonehenge- 6666 km

Stonehenge and Devil's tower- 6666 km

Stonehenge and Bermuda triangle- 6666 km

Bermuda triangle and Easter island- 6666 km

Easter island and Tazumal- 6666 km

"Well, that's not all." said Vikram in a deep voice.

"Let us talk about the time when there were no continents, there was a huge piece of land floating on the water bodies of the earth, called the 'Pangea' the places you saw right now when connected made a star formation and in between stood Kailash, this pattern is similar to the pattern of the Shiv Yantra. Proving that Kailash is the pivotal point of Earth."

"It's very inter-" Epsita was interrupted while she was speaking by a loud thud on the backyard's door.

Vikram smirked and said," So Epsita, what about we both drop our act."

Right after he said that he injected Fentanyl with intense pressure on Epsita's neck.

Epsita fainted right after the dose.

"Raunav! Pick her up and move to the flirine!" Vikram commanded, hurriedly.

Oh well, it is very certain now, that the person behind the loud thud on the door was Raunav.

Raunav with the help of Vikram held Epsita in his hand and rushed towards the flirine and layed her down on the seat and sat on the seat opposite to her. She was still lying unconscious. While Vikram went further to drive the flirine.

While the three were making their way

towards their destination which was only known to Vikram and Raunav,

Vikram exclaimed "That was a pretty hard kick to knock off a door made with such fine and brawny wood!"

"Guru Ji (Shukracharya) has been focusing Astra Vidya too much lately and for some reason he also teaches me kalarippayattu (Indian form of martial arts). So, that is where I got from." Panting from all the commotion said Raunav.

Raunav was slim, had a sharp nose, fair Indian complexion, green eyes, and wavy hair, which made him quite attractive. But no matter how attractive a criminal is, he stays ugly inside. But was it the same case with Raunav, was he really an evil soul or just forced to conduct these unknown willful intentions?

Vikram and Raunav stopped at a point and landed back on the ground, to fetch themselves some snack as it was going to be a long journey from Delhi to Roop Kund.

They sat back in the flirine.

Raunav after a while could no longer bear how such a lovely lady resting near him was in such a miserable condition. So, he untied the cloth tied around Epsita's hands and before he could know, a sudden tight slap hit his cheek, leaving his face as red as a tomato.

Vikram then burst into tears of laughter and started laughing uncontrollably. Epsita exclaimed "Where on earth are you taking me misters!?!?!?!" Is this the way to treat a woman?"

Raunav who was still recovering, replied "First of all, we aren't going to anywhere on earth, it's a place beyond humanity could reach, moreover we are just obeying the orders given by our master and doi- "

"Shut up! I have heard that excuse a billion times." exclaimed Epsita furiously.

"Wait a minute, Epsita? "Said Raunav

"What the hell?!?! You know my name, you stalker!" said Epsita enraged

"Epsita I am Raunav, remember?"

"Huh? Oh my god, why did it have to be my best friend who is abducting me." Groaned Epsita

"Vikram! Why didn't you tell me that the woman was Epsita?"

"How on earth would I have known that you know each-other?!?" said a confused Vikram

"How do you both know each-other?"

"It's a long story…………." Replied Raunav

CHAPTER 6

OLD FEUDS

Old feuds

"And complicated" added Epsita.

"Yes" said Raunav.

"So, what exactly happened I'm extremely curious." Asked Vikram

"So, listen Narottam, many yea- "Raunav was interrupted.

"Narrottam! Like the one in the story Vikram told me. Who is Narrottam?" Shouted Epsita furiously.

"I am," said Vikram.

"Why am I getting to know all this just yet?!" clamored Epsita.

"I guess Vikram here, didn't seem to give it enough importance to update you about all this." said Raunav.

"But let's skip that for now and not do the same thing Vikram did to you by not informing me." He requested Epsita.

"So, Vikram as I was saying, me and Epsita were friendly companions or were each-other's shadows. We both enjoyed each other's company and noticed how our outlooks and our lifestyle had many similarities. But now a question arises, were we just friends or even just best friends? Well, we both never figured that one out. What I always thought was that: we both loved each other but never really thought of taking it further. In addition to this, the strange happenings that I had to undergo had an impact on Epsita's life too. Which I did not want, so I left her and never met again. No information, no reason, no explanation whatsoever I just left and never really showed up again. Was I a coward or was I too protective over my 'friend'?" he said.

"It was really too complex what we were to each-other" sighed Epsita.

"Moreover, what were the strange happening did you ever figure out?" she added.

"You'll figure it out when we reach our destination" said Raunav.

"Anyhow, I'll tell you my part, it was the time when I was just having some food while talking to you (Raunav) and I had something in my mind." She took a pause unexpectedly.

"And it was?" Raunav smirked as if he knew what was about to come out of Epsita's mouth.

"For a minute, when you were looking straight in my eye, my life took a pause, I felt nothing but a sense of connection with you. It felt as if we had known each other for years or maybe lives, I had fallen into you completely, I could hardly control myself, when you bid me farewell for some trip you were going on and never came back. I thought I had nothing to live for, no one there for me, no one to support me. I was lonely, living on a riverside of roopkund for God knows what, until it was Kaliyuga, and I met Nisha and Vikram, who guided me and showed me something I could live for; ARCHAELOGY." Epsita said.

"Wait! What? Miss, did you like me? Huh? But isn't it that we promised each other that we will not fall in love with each other?" Raunav was definitely not ready to accept the fact that he liked Epsita Infront of her.

Epsita felt embarrassed of the fact that she showed her affection towards Raunav.

And so, she replied, "I know, and I never said that I liked you, you are my best friend and nothing else to me, the incident I told you about was just a 2-minute attraction, plus you look so cringe."

Raunav did not realize that she just lied and Raunav believed her instantly.

Since it was a long journey, Vikram stopped the flirine in a safe place and said," Guys! It is quite dark now and I don't feel right to go any further so we shall rest and continue tomorrow morning."

After such a long argument Epsita instantly slept on Raunav's shoulder, which gave him butterflies but didn't express it and slept too, leaning his head towards the flirine's window.

It was exactly 12 am when Epsita woke up and sat with her spinal cord straight and looked around her when she found Raunav sleeping with his head leaning on to the flirine's window.

She couldn't control herself after seeing her friend sleeping like this from laughing and whispered, "He thinks I don't know anything."

Raunav woke up too and found Epsita already staring at him.

"What?" Epsita asked as if she didn't do anything and behaved unaware.

"Nothing! I just realized how cringe you look on your Dp with that weird pout." Raunav whispered so that his voice doesn't wake up Vikram.

Epsita instantly removed her profile picture and said, "Why do you care?"

"I don't know about me, but you seem to care enough to remove your picture and stop my eyes from bleeding." Raunav smirked and said these rude words.

They both went out of the flirine which was on the land after 5 continuous hours.

"Doesn't this starry night remind you of something, Epsita?" Raunav asked while gazing at the sky.

Old feuds

"What?" Epsita asked while searching for something.

"Can't you ever just ask me what you want?" Raunav reacted when he found out Epsita was looking for something and handed over his water bottle to her.

"How did u get to know that I was thirsty?" Epsita asked in utter bafflement.

Raunav thought, "Isn't it what you call love?"

But instead of this he said, "Experience, you know."

Even after Epsita couldn't really find any sense made, she still thanked him.

They both totally forgot about what they were talking about and sat beside each other, admiring the beauty of the night sky.

Raunav asked," Epsita, do you remember during 2023 we used to be such great friends?"

Epsita said," But you literally left to your so-called trip during Satyuga how would I even meet you afterwards?"

Now are you all thinking that, how can Epsita be alive, if she was there in Satyuga too?

To be continued……

CHAPTER 7

THE DIVINE METAMORPHOSIS

The divine metamorphosis

*W*ell, to answer this we need to recall back to the story where; Lord shiva threw the nine gems into the lake at that moment Shukracharya couldn't really pick them up but he did note each incident taking place or rather stalked the location of the gemstones. During his conquest, he saw a fish eating up four of the gems out of the 9 gemstones which were thrown and so that fish transformed into a lady who basically was an epitome of elegance and perfection.

"I never really went away from you" Raunav replied.

"Why the hell am I not aware of this?" Epsita questioned.

"You know that you transformed into a lady from a body of a fish, but I still was a human, way before you. I was 'Bhargav' the one who retrieved information about the Mrit Sanjeevani Vidya from Shukracharya himself." Raunav replied while unfurling his secrets to his love of his life.

Before Epsita could ask any further, Vikram screamed and called them back to the flirine as it was 4 am already...

"Man! Time slips away quite quickly." Raunav exclaimed.

They both sat back and the flirine took off.

Destination was still 6 hours away, which made space for many other conversations.

"So, Epsita, I hope you enjoyed Raunav's company, oh well! Why wouldn't you, you are old friends anyways." Vikram laughed and spoke.

Epsita sat quietly and spoke nothing in reply.

Raunav felt that there was something wrong with her and asked d while touching Epsita's hand," Chhaya, are you okay? I know you might be mad at me for not telling you this earl-"

Epsita moved her hand away from Raunav's and said," Shut up! I don't care about your shit anymore; you don't even consider me worthy enough to know your secrets, what am I? Huh? A bitch?"

Raunav felt ashamed and didn't react any further.

"Bro! Your wifey is mad at you." Vikram mocked Raunav.

Epsita was indeed mad at Raunav, but she still couldn't stop herself from saving Raunav from embarrassment and replied on behalf of Raunav," What makes you so jealous? Oh, sorry bro I forgot you don't have any wifey to be mad at you."

Raunav smirked and Vikram was sulking after such a hard hit on his joke.

Raunav kept his hand on Vikram's shoulder and whispered," Don't offend your sister-in-law, or you would be facing consequences."

The divine metamorphosis

Vikram looked at Raunav and whispered back," True bro, she's fire, take care of her or you will burn."

Raunav sat back as they finally reached their destination.

As the flirine landed, Vikram went out and checked if their way was clear. Once, he was done with all the necessary stuff to be done he shouted and asked Raunav and Epsita to come out.

Both Raunav and Vikram were ready with their winter wear and tents to survive 4 nights there on the lakeside of roopkund.

"You guys kidnapped me, where the hell do you think am I going to get my tent and heavy winter wear it is literally –10 Degree Celsius right now."

"You can come in my tent it is big enough to fit 4 people in here." Raunav offered.

Epsita gave a disappointed expression but was incredibly happy inside her own thoughts.

While Raunav too had the same feeling as Epsita agreed to stay with him in the tent.

Raunav now had a chance to elaborate on all the things he had been hiding from Epsita.

After setting up the tents and ensuring that they would stay in their place no matter how strong air currents were,

Epsita sat in the tent with five layers of jackets to prevent the frigid wind from affecting her.

Not only the cold was awful but also the fact that Epsita was still clueless about what she was here for, which made it even more searing for her to control her emotions.

Raunav was jobbing his clock when suddenly Vikram rushed into their tents and exclaimed "Change of plans! The sarsens are coming in an hour!!!"

"But why and who in earth told you that?" said Raunav.

"Why do you care? Just mind what I told you." Vikram warned.

"Crazy scoundrel" Raunav murmured.

"Sarsens? Are these the ones which are standing as pillars in area of Stonehenge?" Epsita tried to confirm.

"Yeah! You are right." Raunav reassured.

"But they are situated in U.K. you idiot, how will they come to India? Do they have legs?" Epsita asked in sarcasm.

"Because they are living, they have been standing at one place for yugas, it is time to free them from the curse of Arjuna." Raunav calmly replied.

"What, what are you all up to? What am I not aware of? And is it the same arjuna from Mahabharata? Epsita was baffled and asked multiple questions in a queue.

While Raunav was busy hiding a few secrets from Epsita, Vikram created a circle on a large scale with the help of Sindoor.

You might be confused, "Why was Vikram making a circle with Sindoor and why was Raunav hiding his true intentions?" But that is not really the thing to be known right now as there was someone else behind all these activities.

A wild guess?

Oh, well it was Shukracharya himself, who was keeping an eye on each one of them from mount Kailash itself.

"Okay Epsita! Fine I'll tell you." Raunav's patience had crossed the threshold and he finally started to unfurl the secrets he was hiding from Epsita.

"We guys are here at the lakeside of Roopkund just to activate one of the 9 gemstones, the 'Kaal Ratna'." Raunav whispered so that Vikram doesn't get to know that the secret has been already disclosed.

"So, why do you guys need me over here?" Epsita asked.

Raunav answered her, "It is because you have 4 gemstones in your body right now without which the Kaal Ratna won't reveal itself."

"Okay, so why were you hiding it from me? I mean why do you even want those gemstones?" Epsita was a bit skeptical.

"Because we are working for Guru Shukracharya, and without you we won't be able to help him." Raunav replied.

"You call me your friend and you are using me for your dangerous motive to help that villain." Epsita spoke with an emotional voice.

Raunav wiped the tear which was trickling down Epsita's cheek and said, "I am forced to."

"WHY??" Epsita asked another question.

"You know I am Bhargav and not Raunav right?" Raunav asked.

"Yeah so?" Epsita replied.

"It was Satyuga when you weren't like this, in fact you didn't even exist. I used to be an ordinary teacher in a Gurukul, with extraordinary information about all Vidyas. Shukracharya was sulking on the pathways of the village of Nirayana, situated near the Himalayan range, when I saw his miserable condition and asked him to come at my place and tell me his introduction. As soon as we reached back at my home, my hand was paralyzed, I couldn't pick it up, and then the sage I took to my place turned my face towards him and hypnotized me, he made me do awful things to the locals and the animals, he made me Tamsi (A person addicted to flesh.). I killed many, ate their flesh and got addicted to such crimes. I wanted to be freed, but for that I had to promise Shukracharya that till the time he doesn't receive his Mrit Sanjeevani Vidya, I won't leave him. Instantly after that promise I was freed from the hypnotism, I still get nightmares of the dirty scene I saw, the miserable condition of my face; blood smushed all over my mouth, my eyes filled with fire to kill many others which slowly subsided once the effect of his hypnotism broke." Raunav lowered his head and told his story which was filled with miseries and horror.

"I'm sorry to hear that" mournfully said Epsita.

Before any further conversations between Epsita and Raunav, they felt the ground beneath them shaking.

"They have arrived." Raunav gave a hopeful smile.

CHAPTER 8

THE ARRIVAL

The Arrival

𝒱ikram stepped away from the border of Sindoor he just made, and without wasting a second Raunav and Epsita also came out of their tent to see what had just happened, when they saw huge vertical and long pieces of rocks landing in the circle one by one from the sky.

"What the -" Epsita was out of words after seeing such a mesmerizing view.

Raunav bowed Infront of those rocks and sat on his knees.

So, now you might know that these rocks were nothing but the Sarsens of Stonehenge.

Raunav started to speak in a mighty manner.

"O' dear Sarsens, we are the followers of Guru Shukracharya. I am Bhargav, He himself is the great Narottam and she herself is The *Ratnamatsyam (The fish who owned four of the legendary gems.) who is now Ratnima (The lady possessor of the gems).* We are here to navigate our way to The Kaal Ratna which I suppose is of foremost importance to gain the powers of Mrit Sanjeevani. And I can suppose thee, and thy army have arrived for the search of the auspicious gem holding the darkest stream of the almighty Mrit Sanjeevani Vidya. Which would help you to regain your body and break the curse given by the mighty warrior arjuna."

"How do we know that you now keep the power and don't use for your own needs and that you are really with Shukracharya?" Said one the Sarsens.

"You must trust us, as we called you here on this lakeside of Roopkund in order to break your curse and retrieve our first mantra from the Kaal Ratna and unlock the first stream out of the nine." Said Raunav.

"We believe you and hence, order you and Ratnima to get ready for the crescent moon night, where Ratnamatsyam. will have to gift one drop of her blood to the key portion of Roopkund to request the gem to come out and prove that we are accompanied with the others ratnas and call out the kaal Ratna from the depths of the lake." Ordered one of the Sarsens.

3 Days Later.......

It was finally the night when the crescent moon appeared clearly in the night sky, reflecting its bright light all over Roopkund. The light that makes Kaal Ratna enter the realm of land and visit this planet just under the residal of its creator. This is the night when Lord Shiva performed the Shiv Tandava which created havoc in all the three realms just to divide the nine streams of Mrit Sanjeevani Vidya which left the most prominent one closest to his residal: The Kaal Ratna was created, which held the dark arts of Mrit Sanjeevani Vidya, an art that only few people could learn. The other gems spread on the planet as mentioned earlier which had existed in a fish's body who took the form of a human as Epsita.

The three knew that the Kaal Ratna would only dare to come in this realm if other gems like itself have existed here. The blood of the fish was the only way to achieve this goal. So, eventually the gems would need to come out, that have resided in Epsita's body and made the woman immortal.

At 12 am, the time before the rise of the sun or also known as the only time the Kaal Ratna can exist on our realm, Epsita brought a blade to slit her index finger, which would produce some blood to be put in the middle of the lake of Roopkund. Once Raunav, planted the drop of blood over there, mass amount of light was produced this light was no other than the light of the gem, Sarsens were shining bright in blue and green, some reflections of the light reflected on the slit on Epsita's index finger which recovered it completely not even a single spot was to be seen.

All the light was then absorbed by Raunav, his right hand was still shining bright in all the colors of the night sky, which amazed Epsita, but before she could say anything, The sarsens broke one by one, leaving a few dust particles behind, which clearly meant that Raunav lied to the Sarsens about freeing them from the curse instead they destroyed and reduced to dust. Did the sarsens attain salvation? Did they escape their fate by breaking the curse? Had they never been there? How on earth had they just disappeared even after the fact that the Kaal Ratna had come at exactly the time it had to? What had gone wrong?

CHAPTER 9

THE TAX OF LOVE

*I*n the dead of night, the time of the *kaalratnasya kaal (the time of the Kaal Ratna)* the gem came out shining brightly. In such a bright light that blinded the three whom were to possess the shiny rock.

"Now what do we do?" asked Vikram.

"Narottam! You are accompanied by the powers of our guru. You are going to be the one who will attain this gem and give it to our master. The powers of the sarsens are bound to be useless in front of this mighty gem. This power is beyond human comprehension. But you are not supposed to be a human from Satyuga. You are Narottam, the follower of the evil!" shouted Bhargav in all the havoc.

Before the last Sarsen could break, it cursed Raunav saying,

"कालरत्नप्राप्त्यर्थं एतत् पवित्रं कार्यं मनुष्याणां कृते कस्मिन् अपि युगे असम्भवं जातम्। एषः सच्चिदानन्दसहितः सच्चिदानन्दः । परन्तु एषः प्रेम्णः दीर्घकालं यावत् न स्थास्यति। अहं भवन्तौ शापयामि यत् भवन्तौ कदापि परस्परं न भविष्यतः।"

("This holy task to attain the Kaal Ratna has been impossible for humans in any era. This is true determination accompanied by true love. But this love will not last for long. I curse you both that you both will never be each-other's.")

As the Sarsen broke into pieces and then finally to dust, Raunav smirked and said "This isn't what you call love. Dipshit!" comforting himself.

Epsita, who was still noticing all of this, felt bad as she genuinely loved Raunav, and since he was cursed, she thought what if her true love leaves her? Or maybe something negative happens.

Apart from all this commotion, there still was another secret hidden by Epsita.

What was it?

Well, we would be knowing that in the next day's night.

"Epsita, you saw how that loser simply cursed me without knowing that I don't have any true love." Said Raunav, addressing Epsita.

But as of now there was no time left for any conversation. There were only 39 minutes left till sunrise and then the Kaal Ratna would not come to this realm for the next millennium. Remembering the terror and fear of being embraced in pure torture, Raunav didn't delay even a second and grabbed the Kaal Ratna which was floating in the air, amidst all the light. Remembering the terror and fear of being embraced in pure torture, Vikram quickly snatched the gemstone from Raunav's hand and asked him to get back to his tent.

Raunav was pissed by Vikram's behavior but couldn't utter a single word against him and got back to his tent.

It was 3 am when Vikram once again came into Epsita and Raunav's tent, just to wake them up.

"My fellow mates! Get up!" shouted Vikram.

"Why the hell, can't you stop disturbing Vikram." said Raunav in an agitated tone.

Before any other word to be uttered by Vikram,

Epsita and Raunav suddenly felt a horrifying shock. The earth was trembling.

"What is happening? Raunav?" asked Epsita.

"The Shiv Tandava!!" Answered Vikram

The fact that a semi-human possesses such a powerful stone is causing havoc in all the three realms. While creating the apex amount of havoc in lord Shiva's realm, the trios now had to find the mantra to activate The Kaal Ratna they had. But how?

"Vikram, do you hear that?" asked Raunav.

"Of Course, I do!" Exclaimed Vikram

"It's time! The time when Lord shiva disclosed the mantra lock of Kaal Ratna." said Vikram.

"And because we have the Kaal Ratna with us, there is a large amount of commotion created between the three realms, causing Lord shiva to perform Tandava. Vikram you are not just an ordinary man from the Satyuga, you are the great evil-follower, it's time for you to pierce into the center of Roopkund and attain the mantra to activate the Kaal Ratna before the skeletons come out to protect the mantra and eat us alive. These skeletons are none other than the protectors of the gem we have in our hands

As Raunav and Vikram concocted a devastating evil plan, The Shiv Tandava Stotra then echoed all over the valleys and the sky.

**जटा टवी गलज्जलप्रवाह पावितस्थले गलेऽव लम्ब्यलम्बितां भुजंगतुंग मालिकाम्।
डमड्डुमड्डुमड्डुमन्त्रिनाद वड्डुमर्वयं चकारचण्डताण्डवं तनोतु नः शिवः शिवम् ॥१॥**

Due to the high frequency of the Stotram, an unexpected Avalanche occurred, taking away each and everything which came in its way.

**जटाकटा हसंभ्रम भ्रमन्त्रिलिंपनिर्झरी विलोलवीचिवल्लरी विराजमानमूर्धनि।
धगद्धगद्धगज्ज्वल ल्ललाटपट्टपावके किशोरचंद्रशेखरे रतिः प्रतिक्षणं ममः ॥२॥**

Even after the intense pressure of the avalanche Vikram and Raunav, somehow pierced through it and tried to reach the frozen skeleton lake (Roopkund). At the same time, Epsita packed some necessary tools kept in Raunav's backpack and followed the two.

> धराधरेंद्रनंदिनी विलासबन्धुबन्धुर स्फुरद्दिगंतसंतति
> प्रमोद मानमानसे।
> कृपाकटाक्षधोरणी निरुद्धदुर्धरापदि क्वचिद्दिगम्बरे
> मनोविनोदमेतु वस्तुनि ॥३॥

"Raunav keep on holding me tightly with the help of this rope." said Vikram, passing Raunav a rope tied to himself.

Vikram slowly stepped forward as the pressure increased and the temperature dropped.

> जटाभुजंगपिंगल स्फुरत्फणामणिप्रभा कदंबकुंकुमद्रव
> प्रलिप्तदिग्व धूमुखे।
> मदांधसिंधु रस्फुरत्वगुत्तरीयमेदुरे मनोविनोददृतं
> बिंभर्तुभूत भर्तरि ॥४॥

"Hey who is that?" Vikram shouted.

> सहस्रलोचन प्रभृत्यशेषलेखशेखर प्रसूनधूलिधोरणी
> विधूसरां घ्रिपीठभूः।
>
> भुजंगराजमालया निबद्धजाटजूटकः श्रियैचिरायजायतां
> चकोरबंधुशेखरः ॥५॥

"Epsita!!! No not her." Raunav screamed in a worried tone.

"Why is she going the opposite direction." Vikram asked while stopping near the epicenter of the avalanche.

ललाटचत्वरज्वल द्धनंजयस्फुलिंगभा निपीतपंच
सायकंनम त्रिलिंपनायकम्।

सुधामयूखलेखया विराजमानशेखरं महाकपालिसंपदे
शिरोजटालमस्तुनः ॥६॥

Vikram untied himself and left Raunav alone in the middle of all the havoc, he then headed towards Epsita.

"Epsita!! Don't go there, it's not safe, come back! It's my order!" Vikram shouted from far away while running towards her.

Even after Vikram shouted multiple times, she still went towards a dark cave taking off all the jackets she had covered herself with.

करालभालपट्टिका धगद्धगद्धगज्ज्वल द्धनंजया
धरीकृतप्रचंड पंचसायके।

धराधरेंद्रनंदिनी कुचाग्रचित्रपत्र कप्रकल्पनैकशिल्पिनी
त्रिलोचनेरतिर्मम ॥७॥

Are you still wondering what made Epsita do such a weird behavior?

It was due to Hypothermia, which caused her to hallucinate Vikram and Raunav as sarsens from whom she ran away into a dark cave and due to hypothermia, itself she thought that she was feeling warm and took off her jackets in such a low temperature.

नवीनमेघमंडली निरुद्धदुर्धरस्फुर त्कुहुनिशीथनीतमः प्रबद्धबद्धकन्धरः। निलिम्पनिर्झरीधरस्तनोतु कृत्तिसिंधुरः कलानिधानबंधुरः श्रियं जगंदुरंधरः ॥८॥

"Epsita come back! You must!" Vikram said, trying to come near her and assure her that he wasn't there to cause any harm to her.

Without delaying a second Epsita pounced on Vikram and bit him on his wrist as he tried to hold her and take her back to the tent safely.

But a question arises. Why was Epsita so petrified of the sarsens?

Hadn't the three defeated the Sarsens?

Some strange feeling hit the back of Vikram's mind. If there was still something which had to happen to Epsita due to her Hypothermia what would happen to the auspicious four gems inside her? They would only get scattered all around the Earth. Which would only make things complex for him and Raunav.

"What the hell? Are you mad! Who bites a person so badly." Vikram screamed while covering the wound from his hand trying to stop the blood's overflow.

Unexpectedly, Vikram realized that the Stotra stopped echoing and everything was back to normal except Epsita, Raunav and their tents.

TO BE CONTINUED ……

CHAPTER 10

THE BETRAYAL

Where Epsita lied down as a corpse and Raunav who achieved the last moments of recollecting the mantra to rejuvenate the Kaal Ratna and fainted, the tent totally uprooted and stuck under the debris, the three were all totally gassed out after the havoc. But in the end, they were indeed able to attain the Kaal Ratna or the gem of dark arts accompanied by the mantra to activate the gem.

All had been settled.

Or had it?

The three were not able to move in any manner and how would they. Such havoc was enough to put anyone in a devastated state of emotions and mind. Such tense havoc has the potential to put an end to one's life.

Vikram who was the only one left conscious and went forward to pick up Epsita, after being successful, he went back to the place where Raunav was still lying unconscious on the snow bed and tied his foot to Epsita's and dragged both to a comparatively warmer place, out of the boundaries of Himalayan range and stopped near Kutumba Vana.

Vikram, being a man of Satyuga, had so much strength That he was able to save both of them from the cold without even a sigh. His strength was unmatched by any living being on the earth. He then uprooted a tree with one blow and lit it up with his lighter, to keep them warm until they regained their consciousness back.

As the darkness got erased by the bright rays of sun, Epsita finally opened her eyes, now without any effect of hypothermia and went to Vikram immediately after recovering.

"Oh Epsita, you recovered! Is Raunav awake too." Vikram exclaimed.

"Narottama, how dare you, let Shukracharya curse me. Huh? I have now gained back my memory. Such pitiful action wasn't expected from you even if it's thousands of years back. I considered you as one who cared about me, who made me the one who I am. But this?!?!" Epsita raged.

"So, at last you were able to break the curse." Vikram said with a change of tone.

Are you all still wondering what is the curse that Epsita and Vikram had been talking about?

To comprehend what the two were discussing, we need to go back to the time when Epsita was a fish also known as *Ratnamatsyam.*

Till now, we know that Epsita's history starts as a fish who mistakenly ate four gems out of 9.

Was it really a mistake or an action taken intentionally?

The Betrayal

Let's go back to the time when Shukracharya was a teen.

He was just like any ordinary boy but what made him different from others was his exceptional presence of mind and the way he easily memorized anything, but there was something which was totally abnormal, his anger which took over him, out of the blue.

It was the time when Shukracharya and his gurukul mates were grasping Maukhik Shiksha as in verbal education, from guru Brihaspati, Shukracharya was sitting at the backmost place on the chatai or mat which was laid on the ground.

A small ant was struggling in carrying the sugar particle, which was lying near Shukracharya, without delaying a second Shukracharya picked the sugar crystal and kept it on the other side where there was a small ant hill. Seeing such kind actions of Shukracharya, Brihaspati knew it quite well that he showed signs of a proper Sanyasi, but unexpectedly, Shukracharya picked the ant and slowly plucked off the limbs of the ant and smushed it on the ground.

Observing such cruel actions of Shukracharya, Brihaspati stood and punished him for his actions by Kesh Shuddhi Karan (A ritual where, the brahmin ponytail at the back of the head is chipped off and is then freed in some holy river.). This news had spread all over the village where

Shukracharya cried innocently and said that he had no idea of what others were blaming him for.

Seeing tears in Shukracharya's eyes his mother believed him instantly and claimed that all the blames were false and that her son was innocent.

Another event took place where Shukracharya was sitting alone under a tree, feeling totally lonely as he had no friends due to his actions, when suddenly a rabbit sat near him. Shukracharya's gentle gaze had fallen on the rabbit, and he tried to pick it up, but the rabbit hopped a meter away from him as if it wanted to play,

Shukracharya started to run after the rabbit, reflecting his innocence, finally the rabbit accepted its defeat and let Shukracharya pick it up. He fed the rabbit some chopped carrots and as soon as the rabbit ate the carrots, Shukracharya picked the rabbit up and snapped its neck, poked its eye sockets with his fingers, and tried to fill them with sand, when he realized that a couple of people were coming to his direction, he made this innocent face and cried for the rabbit's brutal death.

The villagers were already aware of Shukracharya's actions, so, they tied him to a tree and called his family. A sage had been noticing all the havoc from the beginning and so he performed Deh Vibhajita on Shukracharya that evening.

Shukracharya started to shiver and after a couple of minutes, there were two bodies which formed, 1 was of Shukracharya himself and the other of the evil who had been disturbing the tranquility of the village. The nameless being stood Infront of everyone with pure rage and shun cruelty.

Before he could cause any other damage to anyone, He was held tight and was thrown in a dark pit, filled with nothing but air.

Shukracharya was then freed, by which everyone there was satisfied and tension free of any other issue to show up.

The end?

They lived happily ever after?

A BIG NO CAN DO.

Shukracharya grew up into an 18-year-old individual, where he inculcated himself into Meditation and Tapasya.

But what about the other body which came to existence from Shukracharya?

Well, he didn't die.

Shukracharya still had some remains of that evil creature, which transformed as the Vikaras, we now know them as:

Kāma (lust), Krodha (anger), Lobha (greed), Moha (deep emotional attachment), Mātsarya (envy) and Madā (pride, wantonness).

But because Shukracharya was quite spiritual these emotions never showed up.

It was just an ordinary day when Shukracharya finally went for Deeksha to his Guru, but this time he realized that Brihaspati never liked him and rather he loved the Devas and so they were provided with Deeksha without any Pareeksha. Krodha took over Shukracharya and then he decided to meet the one who was longing for flesh, blood, and violence for all these years.

It was time near the sunset when Shukracharya left his home in search for Kaal Vana where the Evil was trapped.

As soon as he reached it, he heard a ferocious growl echoing throughout the forest, it was coming from the pit's direction.

Shukracharya followed the sound and finally reached the pit which was covered with a piece of flat rock hooked to the ground firmly.

That area wasn't travelled to or visited to, due to the presence of this pit, which made it look awful and unmaintained.

Shukracharya, being the brightest student of Brihaspati knew how to destroy or lift heavy things, and so he picked up a twig from the forest bed and spoke out some mantras which transformed that twig into a powerful weapon, with its help Shukracharya lifted that rock with ease.

After the rock being pulled out came out a zombie like man out of the pit, with worn out clothes, long beard, wounds filled with pus, nails totally filthy and plaque filled teeth.

Shukracharya's eyes scanned his dreadful looking body in seconds and so he said," I am not here to cause you anymore harm. I need vengeance by seeking your help."

The man said in reply," Even if you are here to harm me you won't be able to, you know I am already powerful enough to turn you into ashes with one blow."

"I am not here for arguments; I am here to help you." said Shukracharya with slight arrogance.

"And how would you do that?" said the man.

"We'll see about that later, but what is important for me to do first is taking you to Sushruta so that he cures your ugly looking wounds." said Shukracharya in disgust.

"It's Amavasya, and Indra Doot would be coming this way to go to Sushruta and Dhanvantri, as he has Indra's message of taking back Amrit, and you are going to kill that Doot, so that I can take his place and go to Sushruta with you and the message." Shukracharya said, concocting a well-crafted plan.

It was finally the time to put the plan into action and so, both of them hid behind a bush, waiting for the messenger to come that way.

As they observed a person coming their direction, the nameless man pounced on the messenger, like a carnivore. The blood of the Doot splattered all over the place. The fierce claws and the utter strength of the nameless person or rather creature was unmatched by any creature known to humanity.

After tearing apart the skin on the stomach area of the Doot, he took out the coiled-up intestine as if a string and ate it ruthlessly.

Once he finished eating up the remains of the Doot, he looked in the direction of Shukracharya in hope of further orders.

Shukracharya was well-aware of the man's nature but, he still made an expression of disgust and said," Since, you have no name, from today I give you the Doot's name, 'Narottama'."

"Narottama, it is then." said the newly named, Narottama.

"We head towards Himalaya." Shukracharya ordered.

Narottama nodded and they both started their journey.

2 Days later...

It was finally the time for what Shukracharya had been waiting for, they finally reached Swarnkot, the place where Dhanvantri with his shishyas resided. It wasn't easy to get through the gates of Swarnkot, no ordinary man could, get in without Dhanvantri's will.

Shukracharya knew the necessary things to be done in order to get in, and so he shouted out loud, "Oh seer open the gates, I Shukracharya and Narottama stand before this door with the message of Devraj Indra."

Just by hearing Indra's name, Dhanvantri opened the gates and gave Shukracharya and Narottama to enter Swarnkot.

"Welcome, Shukracharya and Narrot-, Narottama, what happened to you? Indra dev didn't inform me about this." Dhanvantri said.

Before Narottama could say anything, Shukracharya interrupted and spoke, "oh well, I am now his messenger, there was some false news which reached you mistakenly, Narottama is the person who was infected by many diseases and I Shukracharya is the Indra Doot."

"Oh, I see, what are you waiting for then? Come inside, I'll cure Narottama." Dhanvantri spoke while giving a welcoming smile.

Another set of 2 days passed, Narottama was still recovering, while Shukracharya had his eyes on Sushruta and Dhanvantri's secret conversation about Mrit Sanjeevani Vidya but unfortunately Shukracharya could never figure out what exactly they said.

Narottama gained his original self; he had sharp features with perfect set of teeth and flowing short straight hair.

As he opened his eyes, his gaze had fallen upon the lady who was putting medicine on Narottama's wound.

The lady was none other than Epsita herself.

Narottama for the first time, felt a sense of pure love, the love which is totally unconditional and without any sort of rage, as he tried to get up and sit properly, Epsita held him by his shoulder and asked him to rest and stay where he is, so that the stitches don't open.

Epsita got up from her place and looked back at Narottama, where he was still looking at Epsita and finally their eyes interlocked, and gradually Epsita felt the same way as Narottama did for her, blinking her eyes rapidly she came back to real life and went away to keep the sandalwood bowl in its place.

Noticing both the love birds, there was another person in the room who was smiling experiencing the scenario between Epsita and Narottama.

Who was it?

It was Subodh.

Subodh?? Who was he?

Well, just like Epsita, Subodh was one of the Shishya (student) of Dhanvantri who used to work there.

"Uh huh, look at you, acting like you don't feel anything." Subodh smirked.

Epsita hissed and said," you know me well Subodh, don't let me use my powers on you."

What powers was Epsita talking about?

We shall know this in the upcoming chapter with another remarkable plot twist.

CHAPTER 11

THE UNKNOWN?

The unknown?

"Oh ho, ok! Chillax ma'am." Subodh exclaimed.

"Man, this girl can also become a serpent." Subodh loudly thought.

"Because I am a shapeshifter." Epsita said while exiting from the hut to collect some firewood.

"The hec-, youuuuu can hear my words?" Subodh said, while he lost his breath after what he experienced.

It was pretty cold outside and Subodh, being a normal person, went back inside after taking one step outside and experiencing the ultimate cold breeze.

Epsita started her quest of searching for dry or partially dry branches, when she saw Narrottam, standing on the edge of the cliff and gazing up, right into the realms of the sky.

Epsita was in a mood of some bad joke and so she tried to give a slight push to Narrottam, unaware of his wrath,

Where unexpectedly Narrottam held her hand from his back and brought Epsita to his place where the tables turned and now Epsita was about to fall down the cliff but luckily Narrottam was still holding her hand.

"Oh, it was you!" Narrottam smiled with a slight guilt and got her on to the safer portion of the cliff.

"I didn't really expect such a great force to act upon me, nice one." Epsita said out of embarrassment.

"Don't you think a man who is much taller than you to be stronger?" Narrottam asked doubtingly.

"Oh, I forgot, you are a new individual here and so you don't know that every person in Swarnkot has some or the other power, I am a shapeshifter, which is the reason of my confidence." Epsita arrogantly said.

"And I, shattered your confidence." Narrottam said while mocking Epsita.

It was the last straw for Epsita and as Narrottam had already added fuel to the fire he had no option but to face the music.

Epsita turned into an enormous anaconda and wrapped herself around Narrottam, almost choking him until his last breath when Sushrut (Dhanvantri's favorite student) came running to calm down Epsita's anger.

"Epsita, you don't have to punish him, calm down! Guruji cured him and gave him a new life you can't simply snatch it from him." Sushruta pleaded.

Epsita finally found some sense made and she left Narrottam.

"I have my eyes on you, be careful! Cause next time, you won't be standing here." Epsita furiously said, transforming back into a lady.

"What is better than having an angel keeping an eye on me, even I have got my eyes on my prey." Narrottam whispered.

5 nights were away for the full moon to appear which was the perfect time (mahurat) of receiving Amrita from dhanvantri.

"Dinner time guys!" Subodh called out to everyone.

"What is it human or animal flesh?" Narrottam asked.

"What do you mean? Are you Tamsik?" Dhanvantri got offended and questioned Narrottam.

"He is just kidding." Shukracharya tried to cover Narrottam's statement.

"Such kind of jokes aren't used in this yuga! I smell a rat; I am not sure if his thoughts are pure." Said an angered Dhanvantri.

"Guruji, I swear, I have no bad intentions, actually today in the morning Epsita turned into a serpent and serpents don't eat fruits and vegetables, this made me concerned, and I thought to taunt a little." Narrottam added to Shukracharya's statement.

Dhanvantri accepted his excuse but, deep down he was still skeptical about Narrottam's purity.

Narrottam was in a habit of intaking flesh but today was different, as he was sitting beside Satvik people, he couldn't really have any sort of Tamsi food, after taking one morsel of vegetable khichdi, Narrottam dropped on the floor and his mouth started to foam.

Everyone who were their eating food left their plates and made a circle around Narrottam.

Sushruta brought a box filled with medicinal roots and then took out Tagar's root (crepe jasmine) and placed it near Narrottam's nose.

Narrottam got up, straight on his spine and shouted, "THAT'S DISGUSTING!"

Epsita cracked out laughing and said, "Sushruta, he is a newbie, he isn't used to the strong smell of tagar's root or crepe jasmine's root."

Narrottam said, addressing Dhanvantri, "I am really sorry Guruji, but I don't really feel well so, I can't have food."

"It is okay my child, sleep well also, sleep in the room which is besides Epsita's room, over there moon's dim light would fall on your body, which would cool down the acidity in your stomach." Replied Dhanvantri, assuring that Narrottam doesn't feel any discomfort.

The unknown?

"Thank you Guruji." Replied Narrottam in full excitement.

Everybody exited the dinner place and went to their allotted areas to sleep.

Narrottam whispered to himself, "I don't know, but maybe it was my destiny to reach here, no reason of my own or whatsoever, Shukracharya's weird tasks somehow makes me lucky."

"What weird tasks are you talking about?" Epsita said while entering into Narrottam's room.

Narrottam sat up and said, "Is that how you are going to keep an eye on me? Don't tell me you would sleep here."

"Shut up! Will you? Can't you just tell me what I asked." Epsita said irritatingly.

"Alright, I am already aware of your rage. Shukracharya is here for the purpose of taking amrita to Indra dev, right?" Narrottam stated.

"Hmm." Epsita made a sound of agreement.

"Yes so, I was thinking that, why can't he simply take it and give it to Indra dev, it is the fact that I am done with this place, I don't feel like staying here after what you did to me." Narrottam changed his tone from an explanation to regret.

"That's what you think of me? You know I came here to apologize for what I did. You couldn't have been more immature, Narrottam." Epsita said.

"Alright! Fine! I am sorry for saying this, why are you still here?" Narrottam asked.

"I just wanted to leave all our misunderstandings behind and build a new friendship, let us not fight anymore. Ok?" Epsita proposed a deal.

"I have no problem in making friends, why not?" Narrottam answered.

"Okay, great! We'll start another morning with positivity." Epsita said and left the room.

CHAPTER 12

IT IS NOT OVER YET

"*I*t is morning guys! Brahmakaal has started." Said Dhanvantri waking everybody up.

"Everyone is up Guruji." Said Sushruta.

"And I feel more powerful than ever, thank you very much guruji." Said Narrottam, coming back inside in white clothes which were totally wet.

"Oh nice, I am impressed, you have taken a bath much before all my students, very good Narrottam!" Said Dhanvantri in adore.

Epsita wasn't mentally present in that area until….

"What? Haven't you seen someone more handsome than me?" Said Narrottam mocking Epsita's state.

"Stop behaving this dumb Narrottam, I just felt that something very wrong is going to happen." Epsita said in a worried tone.

"It must be just a figment of your imagination, don't worry nothing would happen." Narrottam assured.

"I guess you are right, I am overthinking." Epsita said.

Hours passed and so did the moments of Epsita and Narrottam together.

"It was great fun today, wasn't it Narrottam?" Epsita exclaimed.

Narrottam was still climbing the stone stairs of the steep mountain and said while gasping for air, " y-yes it was a lot of fun." After saying this Narrottam kept the pile of wood he had been carrying on his shoulder and lied down on the ground, breathing heavily.

"That is all? You gave up so quickly." Epsita laughed.

"HAHAHA, very funny." Said a tired Narrottam.

Narrottam quickly got up, back on his foot and asked Epsita to proceed back to home.

When they reached, they found Dhanvantri encouraging Subodh to summon his powers.

"Are you able to see anything?" Dhanvantri asked.

"No guruji, it is totally black." Subodh said, while focusing in between his eyebrows with his eyes closed.

"What are you guys doing?" asked a curious Narrottam.

"They are trying to make Subodh summon his powers." Shukracharya replied.

"He has powers? And he wasn't aware about them?" Narrottam said out of confusion.

Subodh opened his eyes wide open and turned his head towards Narrottam.

"Every person in Swarnkot has special powers, like Epsita is a shapeshifter, Sushruta has high grasping powers and guruji has the powers to create a whole village out of medicines and herbs." Subodh answered Narrottam.

"What powers do you have Subodh?" Narrottam got cautioned and asked.

"I don't know, but as per guruji, I can predict danger or even see something which might be very far from me, basically, I have a supervision." Subodh replied.

Soon Shukracharya's ominous feeling turned into reality.

"Narrottam quick, come over here." Shukracharya whispered into Narrottam's ear in a worried tone.

"We have to get out of here as quick as we can, Subodh is a danger to us. You have a nice bond with Epsita, go and hypnotize her and make her do a sin she can never forget."

"You have never made me happy, Shukra! I was tortured in the pit because of YOU! I am forced to eat this grass-like food because of YOU, and now because of you I have to be separated from my love? That makes no sense, you haven't done anything, for which I am to be tortured once again!" Narrottam clamored.

"ENOUGH OF YOUR SHIT ! What do you mean by being tortured because of me, have I done nothing for you, for which you can do me one more favor to me?" Shukracharya was angered at Narrottam.

"NO, YOU HAVEN'T DONE ANYTHING!" Narrottam backfired.

"Oh really? What about your face? Didn't it get cured because of me?" Shukracharya said in full aggression.

"Shut up! I was always okay with what I had, you got me cured as an excuse of your entry in Swarnkot." Narrottam, once again loudly complained.

"Narrottam, look at me! It is not that I am here to cause any more harm to you." Shukracharya tried to make Narrottam understand.

"Then what is it like? To take your orders? I have a separate life Shukra, you are no one to tell me that, how do I move, what do I do and how to get my shit cured! YOU ARE NO ONE!" Narrottam busted into tears.

"I know I am no one but isn't it important to get you a place you deserve, I am not a boss of yours, neither do I want to be, you definitely deserve more than just Epsita. Anyways she won't come with you until she is impure, isn't that some help?" Shukracharya tried to manipulate Narrottam's decisions.

"Ok then, but only for Epsita, afterwards you may go on your way, and I'll be on mine." Narrottam kept a deal in front of Shukracharya.

"I have no problem with that." Accepted Shukracharya.

"So, what ne-"

"I SEE IT! I just saw something; I swear I did!!"

"Oh no! we are in trouble." Said Narrottam in a sarcasm mixed tone.

"No, we aren't" Shukracharya smirked.

"What do you mean?" Said Narrottam confusingly.

"You will know." Shukracharya said while ignoring to answer.

CHAPTER 13

ANOTHER TRAITOR

Another Traitor

"What did you see Subodh?" asked Epsita in a tone of concern.

"I saw an apple floating in front of my eyes." said Subodh in a sarcastic tone.

"You are so dumb, I thought there was something to be worried about." Said Epsita while not understanding the sarcasm.

"You call me dumb?!?! When you yourself can't understand the sarcasm." Subodh clamored.

Epsita's silence asked Subodh to continue.

"I saw a dark wave, which came towards guruji and took him away from us." Said Subodh in an emotional state.

"What? Me? But how? That isn't possible, I have done nothing wrong to anyone, then how am I to be taken away?" said Dhanvantri.

"Guruji, I think Subodh was just hallucinating, nothing wrong would happen to you." Said Narrottam acting sweetly.

"That is pretty assuring, but I shall ensure all kinds of safety from my side too." Said Dhanvantri while accepting Narrottam's assurance.

It was soon nighttime, when Narrottam and Shukracharya started to concoct a foolproof plan to take Amrit and flee away from Swarnkot.

"What are you guys up to?" Epsita asked vigorously .

"We were planning on how to save guruji from negative energies." Narrottam tried to cover up the situation.

Then Epsita's gaze fell upon the page where it was written:

वयं अमृतं, सम्मोहनं च एप्सिता अपहृत्य ततः अस्माभिः कृतानां सर्वेषां नकारात्मकानां कार्याणां दोषं तां प्राप्नुमः।

"What the holy shit, are you guys doing, and what is this written over here?" Epsita got to know about every wrong intent of the two.

"Cool! Our bait, came to us on her own, Narrottam shall we." Shukracharya smirked, where Narrottam still was struggling in harming Epsita.

"Narrottam, NO! please don't do this to me, I have done everything to keep you happy, please leave me!" Epsita requested while tears trickled down her face.

"I couldn't have been happier to take you away with me, trust me this is the only way we can live together." Said Narrottam coldly.

"Wow! Loved the line Narrottam, now come on stop your love story and make the hypnosis quicker." Said Shukracharya with all his arrogance.

"On it!" replied Narrottam.

Subodh was still witnessing it all but didn't say a word.

Why so? Did Subodh have a fight with Epsita or was he bribed into taking part in this crime?

Well, NONE!

Then what was the reason?

12 hours before this incident…

"Hey Subodh! Could you please come over here for once." Shukracharya called Subodh from the other side of the hut.

"Coming!" Subodh shouted as he neared Shukracharya.

"You called me?"

"Yes, I did, well I had a question regarding Dhanvantri." replied Shukracharya

"Oh, okay, what is it?" Subodh asked curiously.

"Is Sushruta Dhanvantri's son?" asked Shukracharya.

"No, he isn't Dhanvantri's son. Why are you asking this, to me?" asked Subodh with slight frustration.

"Is that so? Well, I was asking that to you because…leave it." said Shukracharya in a devious tone.

This way, Subodh got curious and asked Shukracharya to be clear.

"I don't think you would be able to take it."

"Just be clear, I'll see what to do, myself." Said Subodh in a bold tone.

"As you wish, but please think what you do twice before coming to a conclusion." Said Shukracharya, as he was nearing his goal.

Subodh nodded in agreement.

"Actually, I eavesdropped, Sushruta's and Dhanvantri's conversation, and I got to know that Dhanvantri has been teaching Sushruta a secret form of medical art which may…" Shukracharya was interrupted.

"Oh, so that is what you wanted to inform me? I knew that since years I started working with Guruji. Maybe it is unusual for you but for me and every person who has been working here are used to it. Guruji, is helping Sushruta to complete his book, that's it." Said Subodh explaining the futility of Shukracharya's suspicion.

"Maybe you should hear me out, before saying all that." Said Shukracharya in a tone of request.

"That's not it?" asked Subodh in uncertainty.

"I am afraid, that it is true." Said Shukracharya once again with a whole lot of maneuvering.

"Dhanvantri and Sushruta together are finding a way of forming eternal D.N.A, which cannot be destroyed, according to them you and Epsita are just mere students who work for them, and one day you would be nothing but a guinea pig on whom experiments would be conducted." Said Shukracharya in a devious tone.

"Unbelievable! I don't feel it's true but…" Wept Subodh.

"Sadly, it is true Subodh." Pitied Shukracharya.

"No, I know there is some misunderstanding, this can't be true." Said Subodh confidently.

"I knew it that you won't understand, I came here to help you out, but seems like you don't want to believe me." Said Shukracharya while striking Subodh's vulnerable mental condition.

"Can you really help me?" asked Subodh emotionally.

"Yes, I can" Smirked Shukracharya.

Shukracharya unfurled the plan which he concocted and made Subodh believe that there is nothing wrong in it.

"Alright!" said Subodh accepting Shukracharya's proposal.

_____***End of flashback***_____

Epsita had fallen completely into the hypnosis, which was being conducted by Narrottam.

Shukracharya, stood with his chest filled with air in pride, as his sinful intentions were being fulfilled.

"Accomplished!" said Narrottam smirking in joy.

"Accomplished!" repeated Epsita.

"Isn't that irritating that she would be repeating your words, Narrottam?" asked Shukracharya making an expression of frustration.

"Epsita, please don't repeat my words from now on." Commanded Narrottam.

"Shukra, don't you think you are being a little too fussy in everything? Why don't you try doing something from your side." Grumbled Narrottam.

"Alright, Whatever!" once again Shukracharya in ignorance.

"Tomorrow is the full moon night when we receive Amrit. Make Epsita put poison in everyone's food, tonight we shall capture every person who might stand against us, you got it?"

"Sure, I did." Said Narrottam while accepting the command.

Narrottam, then turned to Epsita and brought his face closer to Epsita's, and said:

"Epsita, end your purity and poison our enemies."

"As you say" said Epsita and headed towards the kitchen.

She added Kaalkoot Visha to the food and served it on the table.

"You took a long time Epsita, where were you?" asked Dhanvantri.

Epsita remained silent and started to look towards Narrottam.

"Actually, she is unable to talk for some reason of which, even I am not aware of." Narrottam closed the topic, knowing that Dhanvantri won't ask anything else.

Morsel after morsel, everyone on the table including Subodh, started to have the food, and remained unaffected for a few minutes, and then the poison started to act on them.

Narrottam loved flesh, and he didn't want to waste any of the flesh which was unpoisoned, so he sat on Sushruta, and slit his neck and separated his head from the body so that he could enjoy, the rest unpoisoned parts.

He slowly started to scoop out all the skin from his claws, and Epsita remained silent throughout the situation and stood helplessly.

Narrottam then came towards Epsita and said, "Smile like you got what you love."

Dhanvantri was witnessing all of this while struggling to speak.

Narrottam then came close to Epsita in the coldest way ever, leaned her to the wall, and whispered, "drink the blood, I would love my wife to have some and relish it."

Narrottam forgot to specify the instructions as a result of which Epsita chose the closest source of blood, Narrottam's blood-stained mouth.

Epsita stood on her toes to reach his mouth and before he could know it, she licked the blood on his lips.

Shukracharya was disgusted by this and said, "I might not want to stay inside for now."

Narrottam started to blush and wanted to feel what he felt again, but he chose to control himself.

Epsita, deep inside her heart was disgusted and was cursing him badly.

Subodh who was still the least affected, cursed Epsita to have no one by her side, when she would be in need.

Another Traitor

Narrottam who was least bothered said, "It's okay, she will still have me."

And as Epsita was commanded to keep smiling, she shamelessly continued to smile.

As the moon subsided and the sun rose, Epsita too started to come out of the hypnosis, and found a blood-stained havoc around her.

She headed towards Shukracharya and Narrottam who were the known cause for this and protested against them.

"Narrottam! How dare you, make me do such a crime, were you out of your mind, did I do nothing for you?!?!"

"I have got more things to oversee, so please just SHUTUP!" said Narrottam rudely.

"Ay, that's my boy, seems like you are growing up." said Shukracharya while mocking Epsita.

"Shukra, you are a prodigy yourself, you are a rishi, how could you remain silent? Why didn't you stop Narrottam, I believed you, I could not even ima…"

Narrottam kept his finger on Epsita's lips, and said, "Don't you remember we got so close, now go cherish it."

"SHUKRA AND NARROTTAM, YOU HAVE DONE ENOUGH AND NOW I'LL SHOW YOU WHAT I CAN DO, IT WAS THE LAST STR…"

"Bla, bla, bla, done? Now let me give you a present." Shukracharya said and picked up Ganga Jal in his right hand and cursed Epsita, into becoming the first animal she sees for 2 thousand years.

Right at that moment, Epsita spotted a fish near the lake and transformed into it.

Narrottam kept himself from rebelling against Shukracharya and stood coldly.

"What a pain in the butt!" said Shukracharya while regretting nothing.

"Amrita is kept in the hut, in a kitchen vessel behind the flour's pot." Shukracharya asked Narrottam to get it, while telling him the exact position of Amrita.

As Narrottam tried to get into the hut but some energy kept both of them from getting inside.

CHAPTER 14

IT'S NOT OVER YET

*T*hat's exactly what Epsita was mad about, and asked Vikram for a reason.

"I am sorry that I couldn't stop Shukracharya, but I had no choice, if you stayed pure, I couldn't have brought you here with me." Said Vikram as an apology.

"I don't care at all now, let it be, but where are we right now? And where is Raunav?" asked Epsita.

As Vikram turned, he spotted Raunav listening to the conversation.

"I can explain…," said Vikram.

"No, it is fine sir, I collaborate with you, where are we supposed to go now?" said Raunav.

Epsita looked towards Raunav in an expression of apology, and Raunav stood emotionlessly and ignored her.

"We head towards, the Chausath Yogini temple in the Morena district of Madhya Pradesh, because we still have a person to wake up."

"What do you mean?" asked Epsita confusingly.

"You will know that in a few moments." replied Vikram.

Nisha then opened her eyes, and found Epsita, Raunav and Vikram sitting on the ground next to her.

And as the cottage's door opened, Shukracharya entered and said, "Good Morning, Subodh."

Now a few questions arise:

who is Nisha? Why did Vikram want to wake her up? In fact, why is Shukracharya addressing Nisha as Subodh?

Well, it is because the story has just started and this is just the beginning, there is a lot more than just a 2-sided love story and invasion.

What more is left is further destruction, energy, horror, and a few heartbreaks.

_____**End of part 1**_____

ACKNOWLEDGEMENT

I am profoundly grateful to my parents, Nani and Nanu whose unwavering love, support, and belief in my abilities have been the cornerstone of my journey as a writer. Your encouragement has been a constant source of strength and inspiration.

A heartfelt thank you to my close friend Arsh Khanna, whose invaluable contributions have added depth and clarity to this book. Your insights and dedication to helping me refine my ideas have been truly instrumental.

To my best friend Samaira, your unwavering belief in me and your relentless motivation has kept me going through the highs and lows of this writing process. Your friendship is a treasure beyond measure.

I extend my appreciation to all those who have supported me along this path, whether through encouragement, feedback, or simply being there to listen. Your presence in my life has made all the difference.

www.ingramcontent.com/pod-product-compliance
Lightning Source LLC
LaVergne TN
LVHW041618070526
838199LV00052B/3196